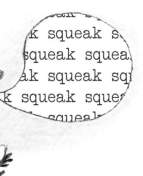

for katie
with love

Tundra Books, an imprint of Penguin Random House Canada Young Readers,
a division of Penguin Random House of Canada Limited

Library and Archives Canada Cataloguing in Publication

Title: Baby squeaks / Anne Hunter.
Names: Hunter, Anne, author.
Identifiers: Canadiana (print) 20200415565 | Canadiana (ebook) 20200415611
ISBN 9780735269095 (hardcover) | ISBN 9780735269101 (EPUB)
Classification: LCC PZ7.H92 Bab 2022 | DDC j813/.6–dc23

Published simultaneously in the United States of America by Tundra Books of Northern New York,
an imprint of Penguin Random House Canada Young Readers, a division of Penguin Random House of Canada Limited

Library of Congress Control Number: 2020951756

Edited by Samantha Swenson
Designed by John Martz
The artwork in this book was rendered in ballpoint pen and colored pencil.
The text was hand lettered.

Printed in China

www.penguinrandomhouse.ca

1 2 3 4 5   26 25 24 23 22

Penguin
Random House
tundra | TUNDRA BOOKS

Anne Hunter

Baby Squeaks

tundra

Baby Mouse was a quiet baby ... at first.

Then, one day, Baby said Baby's first word!

And then Baby said a second!

Baby Mouse talked and talked

. . . and talked.

Mama needed a little quiet.

squeak squeak
squeak squeak
squeak squeak
squeak squeak
squeak squeak
squeak squeak

Baby Mouse met a baby bird!

Baby talked and talked

. . . and talked.

Baby Mouse spied a rabbit.

Baby talked and talked

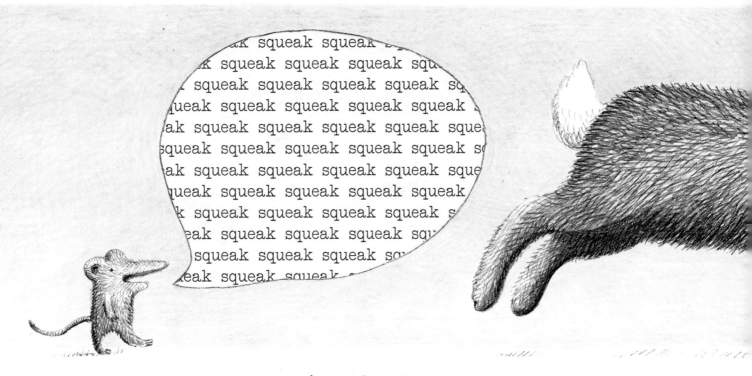

... and talked.

Baby came to a porcupine family.

Baby talked and talked

squeak squeak

... and talked.

Baby Mouse saw a fawn!

Baby talked and talked

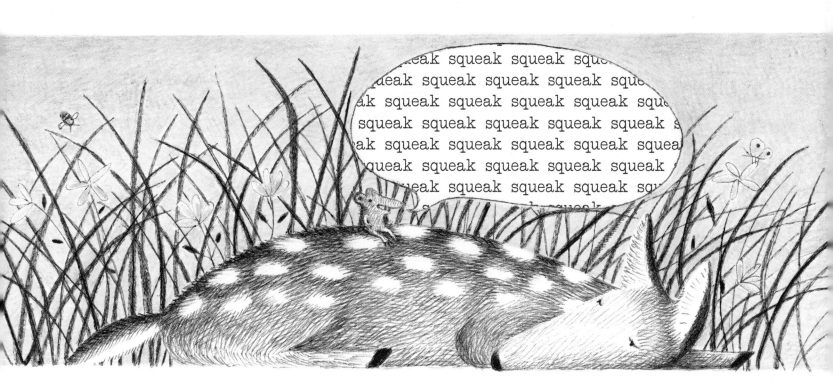

. . . and talked.

squeak squeak

Back at the Mouse house, all was quiet.

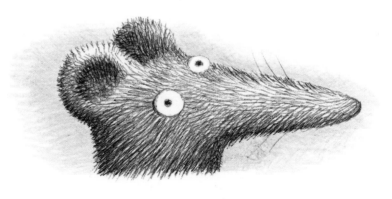

TOO quiet!

Mama Mouse looked
and listened.

Then she heard the sound of
Baby Mouse talking.

Baby talked and talked and talked.

And Mama followed the sound.

squeak squeak squeak squeak squeak squeak squeak squeak
squeak squeak squeak squeak squeak squeak squeak squeak
squeak squeak squeak squeak squeak squeak squeak squeak
squeak squeak squeak squeak squeak squeak squeak squeak
squeak squeak squeak squeak squeak squeak squeak squeak
squeak squeak squeak squeak squeak squeak squeak squeak
squeak squeak squeak squeak squeak squeak squeak
squeak squeak squeak squeak squeak squeak squeak
squeak squeak squeak squeak squeak squeak squeak
squeak squeak squeak squeak squeak squeak
squeak squeak squeak squeak squeak
squeak squeak squeak

squeak squeak squeak squeak squeak squeak squeak squeak squeak squeak squeak squeak squeak squ
squeak squeak squeak squeak squeak squeak squeak squeak squeak squeak squeak squeak squeak s
ak squeak squeak squeak squeak squeak squeak squeak squeak squeak squeak squeak squeak squea
queak squeak squeak squeak squeak squeak squeak squeak squeak squeak squeak squeak squeak sq
ak squeak squeak squeak squeak squeak squeak squeak squeak squeak squeak squeak squeak squea
queak squeak squeak squeak squeak squeak squeak squeak squeak squeak squeak squeak squeak sq
ak squeak squeak squeak squeak squeak squeak squeak squeak squeak squeak squeak squeak squea
queak squeak squeak squeak squeak squeak squeak squeak squeak squeak squeak squeak squeak sq
ak squeak squeak squeak squeak squeak squeak squeak squeak squeak squeak squeak squeak squea
queak squeak squeak squeak squeak squeak squeak squeak squeak squeak squeak squeak squeak sq
ak squeak squeak squeak squeak squeak squeak squeak squeak squeak squeak squeak squeak squea
queak squeak squeak squeak squeak squeak squeak squeak squeak squeak squeak squeak squeak sq
ak squeak squeak squeak squeak squeak squeak squeak squeak squeak squeak squeak squeak squea
queak squeak squeak squeak squeak squeak squeak squeak squeak squeak squeak squeak squeak squeak
ak squeak squeak squeak squeak squeak squeak squeak squeak squeak squeak squeak squeak squea
queak squeak squeak squeak squeak squeak squeak squeak squeak squeak squeak squeak squea
ak squeak squeak squeak squeak squeak squeak squeak squeak squeak squeak squeak sc
queak squeak squeak squeak squeak squeak squeak squeak squeak squeak squea
ak squeak squeak squeak squeak squeak squeak squeak squeak squeak squea
queak squeak squeak squeak squeak squeak squeak squeak squeak squea

Baby was quiet for a moment.

Then Baby talked and talked . . .

. . . and talked.